TWO LOGS CROSSING

TWO LOGS CROSSING

John Haskell's Story

BY

WALTER D. EDMONDS

Illustrated by

TIBOR GERGELY

New York

DODD, MEAD & COMPANY

E760340

PRINTED IN THE UNITED STATES OF AMERICA
BY RICHARD L. JONES, NEW YORK

jE24·1+ω

To

DOROTHY BRYAN
who cut a lot of logs to make this book

FOREWORD

Two Logs Crossing, *John Haskell's Story*, tells how and why a boy grew up to become the man he did. It is a very simple story and it is concerned partly with what other people did for John, but mostly with what John did for himself. And it is also a true story, for, though John Haskell is an imaginary name, there was a boy named Thomas Fortain who learned about crossing his streams in just this way. As a matter of fact, every man who has ever made anything of his life has had to learn to use two logs where two logs are needed. There is no trick and easy way to independence, either for a man or a country.

To be able to do for oneself in one's own way was the dream which first brought some men to this land. There are a few people who confuse it with becoming rich, but money is not the American Dream and never has been. Money can be made of anything you choose, but a man's life is made of the courage, independence, decency and self-respect he learns to use. That was what the Judge, in his own peculiar way, taught John Haskell. And he also taught him that being independent does not mean looking out solely for one's own interest. A man can only be free if his neighbors are also.

Walter D. Edmonds

TWO LOGS CROSSING

Nobody in High Falls had ever put much stock in the Haskell family. They were poor, even in a backwoods settlement like
High Falls, where living came hard. People said that the Haskells
were shiftless. "They don't get anywhere," they said. Charley
Haskell had never stuck to anything, and now it looked as if his
son, John, was going to turn out the same way.

❧[1]❧

He was getting tall for his age. He had outgrown his shirt and his hair needed cutting, but now, as he came along the village road with a string of trout slapping against his bare legs, it didn't occur to him that people might disapprove of him. He had been up the Moose River for two days, fishing the runs below the clefts, and the fish in his string were big ones. When he noticed the people eyeing him, he thought it was because they felt envious of anybody who could bring in fish that size, and he let them slap a little harder against his legs as he approached the store.

There wasn't anything to take him into the store, so he kept on towards home, figuring that he would get there in time for his mother to use some of the fish for dinner. He passed the last house and then the road began to peter out until it was no more than a track in the grass along the riverbank.

The Haskell place stood at the end of it, and the house and barn had a kind of miserable, tumbledown look, even for a poor town like High Falls. About their only advantage was that you could see over the river from the yard between them to Judge Doane's place—if that was an advantage when the roof leaked and the pig fence broke and let the pig into the woods. But John didn't take notice of the looks of the place. His two sisters were on the porch as he came up and he held up his fish for them to see, and when Lissa, who was the next oldest to him, said their mother had been wondering when he would get back, he hung his pole under the porch roof and went inside to the kitchen where their mother was getting dinner.

The brush had been allowed to grow close up to the windows, so the kitchen was kind of a dark room, but with the fire going it seemed all right to John, and he was glad to be home. He slapped the fish on the board beside the dish-pan and said that the biggest would go all of three pounds. His mother said they were fine fish and called Lissa in to help fix them.

Lissa kept swinging one or other of her braids back over her shoulder to keep it out of the way. She was getting almost womanish-looking, John thought, as he sat down beside the table to watch her and their mother cook dinner. Then his brothers came piling into the house to see his fish and ask questions of where he'd got them. Morris said he wanted to be taken along next time, and John said he would take him when he got big enough to walk the ten miles in without sitting down to rest every ten minutes, just the way John's father used to tell him when he was Morris's age.

Then his younger sister, Mary, brought in a load of wood in her plump arms and dumped it in the wood box, and Nat, the baby, woke up and started yelling in the ground floor bedroom, and the cat came out of the bedroom with his tail up, and walked through the kitchen without even noticing the fish and went outdoors, probably looking for a quiet place where he could sleep.

Sitting there with all this business going on around him, John thought his father must have felt the same way at times. It gave him a pleased feeling, like being the head of the family. And then

he noticed that his mother was watching him over the heads of the others, and he had a disturbed idea that there was something she expected of him.

"John," she said. "After dinner I want to have a talk with you."

When Charley Haskell had died that spring, he had left his widow with six children, the four-room house and the rickety barn, the old cow, and a dollar owing from Judge Doane for the sale of a calf.

Mrs. Haskell was a plain, honest, and fairly easygoing woman.

She worked hard enough in the house to keep it and the children's clothes pretty clean, but for outside things she had depended on her husband. And for a few weeks after his death, she had gone on in her old way, letting things ride. But now she had seen that wasn't going to be enough for the family to get along on, and when John came back she knew she would have to have a talk with him.

John was the oldest boy. Morris, who was seven, was the next. In between were the two girls. Mrs. Haskell told John, therefore, that it was up to him to take his father's place towards his brothers and sisters. They looked to him for support, she said, and she depended on him. Then she kissed him a little tearfully, wiped her cheeks with her apron, and took up her existence again exactly where she had left it off when her husband died—as if by a few words she had settled it in the accustomed grooves for an indefinite time.

The sight of her unexpected tears, however, sobered John. He went out of the kitchen and stood a while on the porch. He looked up at his fishing pole once, and then he looked across the yard, where the brown hen and her chickens were picking around in the pigweed, and then he had the idea of going out to look at the cornpatch.

He found it full of weeds. It was an unusual thing for him to get the hoe without being told to, but he did, and after he had cleaned the first row, he found that it looked much better when you could see the corn.

By the time he came in to supper that night, he had a quarter of the field hoed. He called his mother and sisters out to see what he had done and listened with pride as they said it looked nice.

It was while his mother was looking at the corn that she remembered that they had never collected the dollar from the Judge for the calf. She told John that he had better get it that evening.

John said quickly, "I couldn't do that, Ma."

But Mrs. Haskell said he would have to.

"You're the man of the family now," she said. "You've got to tend to the business."

John was frightened at the idea of going to the Judge's house. In 1830, compared to the small houses in the village, the Judge's big stone house across the river was like a palace. John, for one, had never seen the inside of it, but he had seen the lace curtains in the windows and the oil lamps when he went by at night—two or even three of them in the same room, for Judge Doane was the great man of the district. He owned a vast amount of timberland and held mortgages on most of the farms and had been a representative of the county.

John's mother had brushed his coat for him, but even so it looked very shabby and frayed and outgrown as he knocked on the front door and asked the hired girl if he could see the Judge. He had the feeling that it was an impertinence to ask a person like the Judge to pay a dollar, even when he owed it to you. He

thought that probably the Judge would have him thrown out of the house. But his mother had said they needed the dollar for flour and that at least he had to try to get it.

The hired girl left John standing in a front hall that was big enough to put half of the Haskells' house into entire and disappeared down a long passage towards the back. After a while, though, she came back for him, led him to the Judge's office, opened the door, and closed it behind him. John stood with his back to it, holding his hat in both hands, a lanky, overgrown boy, with a thin, rather pale face, and brown frightened eyes. Compared to the Judge, he looked like someone made of splinters.

The Judge's eyes looked cold under the heavy black brows, and he regarded John for a full minute before he said, "Hello, John. What do you want with me?"

But his voice sounded not unfriendly, so John managed, after a couple of attempts, to say that he had come for the dollar for the calf.

"Oh yes," said the Judge. "I'd forgotten about that. I'm sorry."

He heaved himself up from his leather armchair and went to his writing desk and took one end of his gold watch chain from the pocket of his well-filled, speckled waistcoat, and unlocked a drawer. While his back was turned, John was able to see the room, with the impressive lace on the curtains of the windows, the silver plate hung on the chimney piece, and the fire on the hearth, where the Judge burned wood just for the sake of seeing it burn.

The Judge relocked the drawer, replaced the key in his pocket, and handed John a dollar bill. He was a heavy man, and standing close like that, he seemed to loom over John, but in a moment he went back to his chair and told the boy to sit down for a minute. John did so, on the edge of the nearest chair.

"How are you making out?" asked the Judge.

"All right, I guess," answered John. "I wouldn't have bothe you for this, only we had to have it for flour."

"That's all right," said the Judge slowly. "I should have remembered it. I didn't think of it because your father owed me money anyway."

"I didn't know that," said John. He couldn't think of anything to say. He only looked at the Judge and wondered how his father had had the nerve to borrow money from a man like him.

The Judge made an impressive figure before his fire. He was a massive man, with a red face, strong white hair, and uncompromising light blue eyes. He was looking at John, too, rather curiously.

He nodded, after a while, and said, "He owed me forty dollars."

That was what John had wanted to know, but he was so shocked at the amount of it, that all he could do was to repeat, "I didn't know that, sir."

"No," said the Judge, "probably not. He was a kind of cousin of my wife's but we neither of us said much about it. And after Mrs. Doane died he didn't come around much." His brows drew bushily together and he stared into the fire. "How old are you, son?" he asked.

John replied that he was sixteen.

The Judge went on to ask about the family, the age of each child, and what Charley Haskell had got planted that spring. John answered all the questions and as he did he felt a little more confidence. It seemed odd that anyone living in the High Falls settlement could know so little about anyone else. Why, he knew a lot more about the Judge than the Judge did about him. He told how high the corn stood. He said, "It stands as high as any I've seen around here, excepting yours, Judge. And now I've started

looking out for it, maybe it will catch up."

The Judge said, "Hoeing is the best garden fertilizer in the world. And sweat is the next best thing to money."

"Yes, sir," said John. It made him feel proud that he had hoed so much of his corn that day. Tomorrow he'd really get after the piece.

"You can't live on potatoes and corn, though," said the Judge. "What are you going to do?"

John was awed to be talking so familiarly to a man half the town was scared of; a man, it was said, who had even talked out in legislature down in Albany. But his face wrinkled and he managed to grin.

"Work, I guess, sir."

The Judge grunted then, and stood up and dropped his quid into the sandbox.

"You do that and you'll take care of your family all right. Maybe you'll even pay back the forty dollars your father owed me." He held out his hand, which John hardly dared to take. "When do you suppose that'll be?"

John got white.

"I don't know, sir."

The Judge smiled.

"I like that a lot better than easy promises, John."

He walked beside John into the hall, his meaty hand on John's shoulder.

"Good luck to you," he said from the front door.

During the summer John managed to get work from time to time, hiring out for as much as forty cents a day, sometimes as often as three days a week. At first he didn't have much luck getting jobs, for though he was a good deal stronger than he appeared to be, and worked hard, people remembered his father's prejudice against work and preferred getting other help when they could. Besides, in the eighteen thirties, there weren't many people in High Falls who could afford to hire help, even at forty cents a day. So, by working in the evenings and on Sundays also, John had ample time to take care of their corn and potatoes and the garden truck he had planted late.

It used to puzzle him how his father had ever been able to take life so easily. He himself hardly ever found time to go fishing that summer. And once or twice when he did have the time, he thought of the forty dollars he owed Judge Doane and he went out and looked for work instead. He even found occasional jobs at Greig, five miles up the river, and walked back and forth every morning and evening.

Little by little, the forty dollars became an obsession with John, and while at first he had given all his earnings to his mother to spend, he now began to save out a few pennies here and there. When, at the end of August, he had saved out his first complete dollar and held it all at once in his hand, he realized that some day he might pay off the debt; and from there his mind went further, and he began to see that it was even possible that some day he would be able to build a decent house for his mother. Perhaps he'd have his own place, too, and get married; and when the settlement became a town, as they said it would, perhaps he might even get elected to the town board.

By the middle of October, John had saved up enough money to see the family through the winter, as he calculated it, for besides his secret bit, he had persuaded his mother to lay by some of what he gave her. Further, she had been moved by the sight of a decent garden to preserve some beans and also some berries that the girls had gathered, especially since it was the first time in several years that she had felt able to buy sugar ahead of the immediate demand. The potato piece had yielded forty bushels of potatoes; and the corn, which John had sold, had brought in a few dollars more.

The day before he finished cutting the winter wood supply, John counted up his money and decided he would make the first payment on the forty-dollar debt to the Judge that night. It amounted to five dollars, even, but to John that seemed a great deal.

He went up to the big nouse when he felt sure that the Judge would have finished his supper; and he had the same business of knocking and waiting in the hall while the hired girl took his name in. He found the Judge sitting as he had found him the first time, only the fire was about two logs bigger.

"Sit down, John," said the Judge, "and tell me what I can do for you."

John obviously did not know how to begin his business properly, so, after watching him under his brows for a moment, the Judge continued, in his gruff voice, "I may as well tell you I've kind of kept my eye on you this summer, John. I like the way you've taken hold. I'm willing to admit, too, that I was surprised. And I'll be glad to help you out."

John flushed right up to his hair.

"I didn't come to ask for anything, Judge." He fished in his pocket and pulled out his coins. His hands were stiffly clumsy. Some of the coins fell to the floor and one rolled musically all the way under the desk. As he went on his knees to retrieve it, John wished he had had the sense to tie them together, instead of jingling them loosely in his pocket all the way up. He couldn't bear to look at the Judge when he handed him the coins.

The boy said, "I wanted to pay something back on that forty dollars, sir. It's only five dollars, even." The Judge cupped his two hands. "Maybe you'd better count it, sir." But it didn't look like so much in the Judge's hands.

The Judge, however, said, "Quite right, John," and counted up the money. Then he went to his desk, put the money in a drawer, and wrote out a receipt, which he gave to John.

"Yes, sir," said John, wondering what it was.

The Judge looked grave.

"That's a receipt, John. It says you've paid me back five dollars."

John wondered.

"Why," he said, "it's kind of like money, ain't it?"

"In a way," said the Judge, shaking hands. "What are you going to do this winter, John?"

"I don't know, sir. I tried to get a job from Brown at the hotel, splitting firewood, but he's hired Ance instead. Mr. Freel's got all the help he needs at the tannery." Those were about the only winter jobs a man could hope to find in High Falls.

The Judge nodded, and said, "I'd offer you something, if it didn't mean getting rid of someone else, John. I couldn't rightly do that."

"No, sir," John said, and started home.

But somehow, he felt so happy all the way home that when he reached the house and found his mother sitting up in the kitchen, he couldn't help telling her the whole business. He blurted it all out, the way he had saved a little now and then until he had actually got five dollars. And then he showed her the receipt

His mother didn't say a word as she looked at the receipt, but her head gradually bent farther and farther forward and all at once she started crying. John could not understand at first. He thought it might be because she was happy. But she did not cry like a happy person. Finally she lifted her face to him.

"Oh, John, why did you do that?"

"I wanted to pay off that debt Pa laid up," he said, uneasily. "Ain't that all right?"

"I guess it is, John. But why didn't you tell me first?"

"I kind of wanted to surprise you," he mumbled. "I didn't mean for to make you feel bad, Ma."

"It ain't that, John."

"But ain't I give you enough?"

"I didn't tell you either," she said, almost smiling. Then she started crying again. "I'm going to have another baby, John. And I was so proud of you, I didn't say."

"Baby," said John. "Gee, Ma, I didn't know."

She went right on crying.

"But ain't we got enough?" he demanded.

"Oh, yes. You've done fine, John. But the way you've been working has made me feel kind of better. I got to thinking people talked to us different now. I never thought about that before. Sure," she went on, lifting her face. "I'll be all right now. Only when you showed me that about the five dollars, it made me think I could have had a baby that wasn't on the town. I've never had. I don't want to say anything against your father, I loved him. But I never realized before what it would be like to have a baby not on the town. You see," she finished, quite dry-eyed, now, "five dollars would have paid Dr. Slocum and Mrs. Legrand. Two for him and three for her."

Even so, John did not quite understand his mother, except to see that he had taken something desperately precious from her.

As he thought it over during the next two or three days, John felt all torn up in his chest. He began to see that by starting to be respectable, he had done more than just work for himself. He had done something to his mother, too. And now, by paying back the Judge that extra money, he had put her back where she used to be. It did not seem logical, but that was how it was.

Perhaps he would have fallen back then and there to his old ways of letting the world slide, if he hadn't met Seth one evening at the blacksmith's where he had gone to get the big cook kettle mended. Seth was having Jorgen do some work on a few of his beaver traps.

Seth was an Indian. In summer he worked in the sawmills, when it occurred to him to do so, but in the winter he went into the North woods. People distrusted Seth. They did not like the way he smelled. Even in the forge you could smell him, greasy-sweet, through his thick tobacco smoke.

Seth said he was planning to go north in about two weeks. He was late, but the winter looked slow. He thought the furs would be coming up pretty quick, though. Better than last year. Last year he had cleared only two hundred dollars.

Two hundred dollars, thought John. He wondered how a man like Seth could spend all that. All he knew was that the Indian took it to Utica every spring. He supposed there were places in such a big town that an Indian could go to. Two hundred dollars.

He turned shyly to the Indian.

"How much does a man need to get traps and food for the winter?" he asked.

The Indian turned his brown face. He wasn't amused, or he did not show it if he was.

"Seventy-five dollar, maybe. You got a gun?"

John nodded.

"Seventy-five dollars," he thought. He knew only one person

who could stake him that much.

The Indian asked, "You going?"

"Maybe," said John.

"You come wit' me. Good range over mine. Plenty room us both. I help you make a cabin."

"I'll see."

It was almost ten-thirty at night when John reached the Judge's house. He had made up his mind he would ask the Judge if there was a downstairs light still on when he got there. If not, he wouldn't.

The house was dark on the town side, but when John went round to the office window, his heart contracted to see that the

Judge was still up. He tapped on the window. The Judge did not start. He got slowly up and came to the window and opened it to the frosty night. When he saw the boy's white face and large eyes, he said harshly, "What do you want?"

"Please, Judge," said John, "could I talk to you?"

"It's late," said the Judge, staring with his cold blue eyes, for a while. Then he shut the window, and presently opened the front door. He was looking a little less threatening by then, but he wasn't looking friendly.

"Be as quick as you can," he said, when they were back in the office.

John was as white as a person could be. His tongue stuttered.

"I—I wanted to ask you something, Judge. But if you don't like it, say so plain. It's about me and getting to trap this winter on account of that five dollars I paid you." He couldn't think decently straight.

The Judge barked at him.

"Talk plain, boy. Begin at the beginning. What's the five dollars got to do with it?"

John began to talk. He repeated what had happened with his mother, how she felt, how odd it seemed to him, but there it was. The Judge began to sit less stiffly. He even nodded. "Women are the limit," he observed. "You want to take back that money?"

"No, no, *I* don't," John said desperately. "But people don't like giving me work yet, and I want Ma to feel respectable. I thought if you could make me a stake to go trapping——"

"How much?"

"Seth said seventy-five dollars," the boy almost whispered. "But I guess I could get along with fifty. I'd get the traps and some powder and ball, and I could go light on the food. I don't eat a great lot and I'm a handy shot, Judge."

"Seventy-five dollars," said the Judge. "You're asking me to lend that much to a boy, just like that?"

His red face was particularly heavy-looking.

"I'd make it on fifty," said John. "But it was just an idea. If you don't think it's all right, I won't bother you any more."

"Then you want the five back, too, I suppose—makes it forty again. Forty and seventy-five is a hundred and fifteen dollars."

"It would be ninety dollars, wouldn't it, if you give me fifty?"

"Shut up," barked the Judge. "If I'm going to stake you, I'll do it so I'll have a chance of getting my money back. It won't pay me to send you in with so little you'll starve to death before spring, will it?"

John could only gape.

"How about this Seth?" asked the Judge. "He's a drunken brute. Can you trust him?"

"I've met him in the woods," said John. "He's always been nice to me.

The Judge grumbled. He rose and took five dollars from his desk and gave it to John.

"You bring me back that receipt tomorrow night," was all he said.

<§[35]§>

When John gave the money to his mother it made her so happy that he felt wicked to feel so miserable himself. It seemed as if all his summer's work had been burnt with one spark. And he was frightened to go next night to the Judge's house. But he went.

The Judge only kept him a moment.

He took the receipt and gave John another paper.

"Put a cross in the right-hand bottom corner," he directed; and when John had done so, "That is a receipt for seventy-five dollars. Here's the money. Don't lose it going home."

He walked to the door with John and shook hands.

"Good luck. Come here next spring as soon as you get back."

"Thanks," was all John could say.

The Judge made a harsh noise in his throat and fished a chew from his pocket.

"Good-bye," he said.

John got Seth to help select his outfit. The Indian enjoyed doing that. And John felt so proud over his new traps, his powder flask and bullet pouch, and his big basket of provisions, and he felt so grateful to the Indian that he offered to buy him a drink out of the two-shilling bit he had left.

"No drink," said the Indian. "Next spring, oh yes."

He shared his canoe with John up the Moose River and they spent two weeks getting into Seth's range. They dumped his stuff in the little log cabin and moved over the range together to the one Seth had selected for John. There they laid up a small cabin, just like the Indian's, and built a chimney. They had trouble finding clay to seal the cracks, for by then the frost was hard and snow coming regularly each afternoon.

Then Seth took John with him while he laid out his own lines, and after two days went with John, showing him what to start on. After that the Indian spent all his spare time making John snowshoes. He finished them just before the first heavy snow.

John learned a great deal from Seth that fall. First of all he learned that an Indian in the woods is a very different person from an Indian imitating white men. He had always liked Seth, but he had never suspected his generosity and good humor.

Seth seemed to understand how lonely it could get for a boy

living by himself, and during the entire winter he never failed to pay John a weekly visit and ask him back to his cabin in return.

John never figured out which was the best part of that exchange of visits—the sight of Seth coming down the brook shore on a Saturday afternoon, or his own trip the next day over the trail between the cabins. In one way he liked this second part better, for it meant that when he got to Seth's he had nothing to do but sit down and be fed.

It was a six-mile walk that took John up along his own creek for a mile and a half to a low pass between two mountains. Then there was a beech ridge where the bucks had scarred the trees with their horns and fought long battles in the fall. From this ridge the trail went down into an alder swamp and crossed it on the remains of a beaver dam that Seth said had been there when he first came into the country. Why the beaver never returned was a mystery, but the dam was there, an enormously long, curving dyke above the swamp. Only it no longer held water. The stream it used to dam flowed through its ancient course and only the dead stubs of spruces, gray and broken, like old teeth in the alder growth, remained as evidence that once there had been standing water.

From the swamp John climbed another ridge and picked up a small brook on the far side that led him down a long easy grade to the small lake on which Seth's cabin stood. And when he came out on the ice, John would see the smoke rising up from the fringe of cedars, a clear blue finger against the evening sky.

The cabin itself was hidden under the trees, but when he yelped he would hear Seth's yell in return, high-pitched, and far carrying, and a little wild-sounding, especially when the echo came back off the ridge where the pines towered. Then, presently, he would see Seth, brown and shapeless in his old coat, come out on the ice, lifting his arm in greeting, as John approached, grinning round the stem of his old pipe, and taking it out long enough to say, "How, John?" before they shook hands. Then they would go into the cabin, which seemed solid with heat and tobacco smoke and the smell of cured pelts and the steam from the kettle of broth that Seth had on the fire.

Seth was always making broth of some kind—it might have a rabbit in it, or black squirrel, or partridges or even odds and ends, like muskrat, that John would have found it hard to like if he had known of them beforehand, but that seemed all right to Seth. Generally, though, it was a mixture of a good many things and thick and strong, and after his walk through the cold it tasted good to John.

He would admire it, giving Seth great pleasure, and the old Indian would sit back and beam, his broad face suddenly squeezed into innumerable fine wrinklings.

Afterwards they would look at some of Seth's pelts, and talk about their trap lines, and wonder how much money they had made, until it was time for John to start back.

At first he had arranged his visits so that he could get started before dark, but as the winter went on he became so familiar with

his route that he often tackled it after sunset. His snowshoes had packed a hard footing it was easy to follow, even in the dark. The snow had a faint luminance to shape the trees. The night would be full of frost sounds, or he would hear a fox barking on the high slopes, or an owl would hoot him over the pass, and he would occasionally see its dim shape, noiseless as a snowflake in its passing, a dark blot against the stars. The owl lived there all winter and seemed to feel a kind of familiarity towards the boy—as if it looked for his coming. After he got over the first eerie sense of being followed by the disembodied, invisible voice, John came to look for the owl in his turn.

Occasionally he would pick up the sound of his own brook, muffled under the deep snow, and hollow-voiced, where it made small falls between big rocks. This sound of running water came and went beside him until he reached his own cabin under the thick stand of spruce. He would feel his way in and stir up his fire, climb into his bunk and pull his blanket over him, thinking it would be a full week now before he would hear Seth's yell echoing down from the pass and he in turn would go out and wait for the brown figure to come down along the brook.

But that was for the end of the week. Every day John would run one or other of his trap lines. Except for the one he called his home line, that ran down the brook, taking in a couple of beaver colonies, and came back round the small hill, these lines would keep him out till dark, walking hard all the way, when he wasn't re-setting his traps.

It never occurred to him to worry about anything happening to him and he was lucky. He didn't get sick, except for one heavy cold and that came near the end of the week and Seth showed up to look out for him. Seth rigged blankets over a kettle to make what he called a steam lodge. He made John sit naked under the tent of blankets while he dropped hot stones into the kettle from time to time until the steam had the boy pouring sweat. Then the Indian took him out in the snow and rubbed his bare skin with it and dressed him and put him in his bunk and covered him. After that he made him an infusion of some tree bark and roots; he never told John what it was, but it tasted bitter and black and John went to sleep suddenly, his last sight being one of Seth sitting on the floor before the fire, poking wood into it, and smoking his pipe, the smoke of which was sucked into the chimney where it joined the firesmoke, and the creeping, lichen-like fringes of sparks.

Once in a while Seth would give a day to go over one of John's trap lines with him, showing him how to reset this or that trap; whereabouts at the top of a slide to set for otter; how to bait for marten; the best way to make deadfalls. John learned how to build pens for beaver under the ice and sink fresh twigs for bait and when the younger beaver swam in, to drop the closing pole and let them drown.

He learned a lot about foxes, both about their habits, so that he could use their own intelligence to trap them, and also how they could be poisoned. Foxes were vain animals. They could not resist leaving a mark on any isolated pole, and one trick was to set your pole up in the ice of a lake. The fox had to come out to cock a leg, and afterwards he felt so proud he would eat anything and he would crack down the bait right away without a thought.

One thing John never became good at was still-hunting fisher. He shot one, but that was a fluke. The rest of the time he spent trying it was just wasted.

But Seth told him not to worry. Either a man could still-hunt fisher or he could not; there was no shame in not being able.

There were days, of course, when John came in without a single skin, but generally he had something to keep him busy in the evenings. And some times he would work by the firelight until he fell asleep and the cold waked him later, when the fire was just a handful of embers, so dim his own shadow did not show against the log wall. It was lonesome for a boy then, and one night he was so cold and stiff it hardly seemed worth trying to move and he let his eyes close again. But suddenly he came wide awake in a kind of panic and found himself standing up. He never knew what waked him; but years afterwards, when he was an old man, he told one of his grandchildren that every man at least once in his life, anyway, comes close to death, and maybe that was the time.

It was hard work, running trap lines. It was hard work just to live alone in the woods and keep working, even when you have a friend only six miles cross-country. But John did well. Early in March his bale of furs had mounted up so that he had Seth make a special trip over and appraise them. The Indian said that John had more than two hundred dollars' worth. It would depend on the market. By the end of the month he might have two hundred and fifty dollars' worth.

John dug into his flour and made soda biscuits for the Indian. They ate them with a little sugar he had left and Seth spent the night in celebration. They talked a long time about how John would be fixed up to pay off the Judge, not only the stake but also the debt, and even have some money to start the summer on.

Next winter he would make a clear profit. He would put money in the bank.

Seth did not understand what you put money in the bank for—not even when John explained that it was by saving money and laying it up against the future that a man got rich like the Judge. Seth agreed that it was a wonderful thing to have a house like the Judge and hire help; but he still did not see the point of having money you did not use up. Besides, as he said, the Judge didn't like him. "Don't like Indian. Don't like me drunken brute."

"That's it," John said. "You spend your money on likker, Seth. Then you haven't got anything at all."

For a few minutes Seth looked both enlightened and sad. But then he smiled at John.

"I lose money," he said. "Well, then maybe I get some more."

It came to John then that the future meant nothing to Seth. He worked and made money and drank it up and worked again, but it all meant nothing. He was just passing his time that way.

It didn't bother John much, though. Seth was a good friend.

The snow went down quickly. When he woke one morning, John was aware of a faint ticking sound all through the woods. He went out of his cabin and looked round but there was nothing to see. Later, however, the drip from the branches began to dent the snow in the black part of the spruce woods. Seth said maybe it

was the frost working out of the trees, or the first creeping of sap. It came every spring. You didn't know. Maybe it was the little people under the earth getting ready to push the grass up. Or maybe it was just something you heard.

Whatever it was, John began to get restless. He was eager now to leave. He wanted to show his furs; he wanted to sell them, he told Seth, on a young market. Seth nodded. He knew how John felt, and he agreed that if John went now there was a chance he could get across the Moose River on the ice somewhere. But he begged John to wait. There was still two weeks for the fur to hold up well, and he had sometimes made some lucky catches in March.

But John's heart was set on going. He couldn't put his mind on trapping any more. He had done so well already. So finally Seth agreed to come over and help him pack his furs and traps. They had a big feed on about the last of John's grub.

In the morning the boy set out. The Indian walked with him to the end of his own south line, and shook hands.

"You one good boy, John," he said unexpectedly. "You come again next year."

"I will sure," promised John. "Thanks for all you've done for me, Seth. Without you, I wouldn't have done this." He hitched the heavy pack up on his shoulder. "I guess next the Judge, you're about the best friend I ever had."

The Indian's brown face wrinkled all over beneath his battered hat. He made a big gesture with his hand.

"Oh sure," he said. "Big country. Nice company. Plenty furs us both."

He held John's hand.

He said, "Now listen to Seth. *If creeks open, you cut two logs crossing.* You mind Seth. You cut two logs. One log roll. Two logs safe crossing water."

"Yes, sure," agreed John. He wanted to get away. The sun was well up by now."

" 'Bye," said Seth.

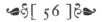

John walked hard. He felt strong, that morning. He felt like a grown man. The weight of the pack, galling his shoulders, was a pleasure to carry.

Every time he eased it one way or another, he thought about what it was going to mean. He thought about coming home and telling his mother. He would buy her a new dress. He would make a purchase of some calico for his sisters. Make a purchase, when you said it that way, was quite a word. He'd never even thought of it before.

He would see the Judge. He imagined himself walking into the Judge's office and dropping the pack on the floor, and looking the Judge in the eye. He realized that this almost meant more to him even than doing things for his family.

He remembered the way he had started the winter. He had asked Seth to estimate the worth of each first pelt. When they had figured up on forty dollars, he had made a bundle of them. They were still packed together in the bottom of the pack. It seemed to him that getting that first forty dollars' worth was twice as much of a job as all the rest afterwards had been.

The snow was a little slushy here and there, but it held up well in the big woods and John made pretty good time. Nights he set himself up a lean-to of cedar and balsam branches, and sitting before his small fire, he would think ahead a few years. He could see himself some day, pretty near like the Judge. He even figured on teaching himself to read and write, write his own name, anyway. No matter how you looked at it, you couldn't make a cross seem like John Haskell, wrote out in full, with big and little letters in it.

Mornings, he started with the first gray light, when the mist was like a twilight on the water and the deer moused along the runways and eyed him, curious as chipmunks. He walked south down the slopes of the hills, across the shadows of the sunrise, when the snow became full of color and the hills ahead wore a bloody purple shadow on their northern faces.

Now and then he heard the first stirring of a small brook under the snow in a sunny place and he found breath holes under falls wide open.

John had grown taller during the winter, and he seemed even lankier, but his eyes were still the boy's eyes of a year ago.

He crossed the Moose River on the ice about where McKeever now is, just at dusk one evening. He had not made as good time that day. The snow had been a good deal softer and his legs ached and the pack weighed down a bit harder than usual. But though the ice had been treacherous close to shore, he had found a crossing place easily enough.

That night, however, as he lay in his lean-to, he heard the river ice begin to work. It went out in the morning with a grinding roar, and built a jam half a mile below his camp.

He saw it with a gay heart as he set out after breakfast. It seemed to him as if it were the most providential thing he ever had heard of. If he had waited another day before starting, he would have found the river open and he would have had to go back to Seth's cabin and wait till the Indian was ready to come out. But as it was, now, he would have only brooks to cross.

There were a good many of them, and most of them were opening. But he found places to cross them, and he had no trouble till afternoon, when he found some running full. They were high with black snow water, several of them so high that he had to go upstream almost a mile to find a place where he could fell a bridge across.

Each time he dropped two logs and went over easily enough. But each time the delay chafed him a little more. By late afternoon, when he was only a few miles from High Falls and began to recognize his landmarks, he came to what he knew was the last creek.

It was a strong stream, with a great force of water, and it was boiling full. Where John happened on it, it began a slide down the steep bank for the river, with one bend and then a straight chute. But it was narrow there, and besides where he stood grew a straight hemlock, long enough to reach across.

Hardly stopping to unload his pack, John set to work with his

axe. The tree fell nicely, just above the water. There was no other tree close by, but John thought about that only for a moment. It was the last creek, he was almost home, and his heart was set on getting there that night. Besides, he had had no trouble on the other crossings. He was sure-footed and in every case he had run across one log.

He gave the tree a kick, but it lay steady, and suddenly he made up his mind to forget what Seth had said. He could get over easy enough and see the Judge that evening.

With his furs on his back, his axe in one hand and his gun in the other, he stepped out on the log. It felt solid as stone under his feet and he went along at a steady pace. The race of water just under the bark meant nothing to John. His head was quite clear and his eyes were on the other side already, and he thought, in his time, he had crossed a lot of logs more rickety than this one.

It was just when he was halfway over that the log rolled without any warning and pitched John into the creek.

The water took hold of him and lugged him straight down and rolled him over and over like a dead pig. He had no chance even to yell. He dropped his gun and axe at the first roll and instinctively tugged at the traps which weighted him so. As he struggled to the top he felt the fur pack slip off. He made a desperate grab for it, but it went away. When he finally washed up on the bend, and crawled out on the snow, he hadn't a thing left but his life.

That seemed worthless to him lying on the snow. He could not even cry about it.

He lay there for perhaps half an hour, while the dusk came in on the river. Finally he got to his feet and searched downstream, poking with a stick along the bottom, though he was hopeless. The creek ran like a millrace down the slope for the river and the chances were a hundred to one that the traps, as well as the furs, had been taken by the strength of water and the slide all the way down to the river.

But John continued his search till nearly dark before he gave up.

By the time he reached High Falls, John had managed to get back just enough of his courage to go straight to the Judge. It was very late, but the office light was still burning, and John knocked and went in. He stood on the hearth, shivering and dripping, but fairly erect, and in a flat, low voice, told the Judge exactly what had happened, even to Seth's parting admonition.

The Judge said never a word till the boy was done. He merely sat studying him from under his bushy white brows. Then he stood up and fetched a glass of hot water with some whiskey in it.

Though the drink seemed to bring back a little life, it only made John more miserable. He waited like a wavering ghost for the Judge to have his say.

But the Judge only advised in his heavy voice: "You'd better go on home. I understand you have a new sister. You'd better start hunting work tomorrow." His voice became gruffer. "Everybody has to learn things. It's been bad luck for us both that you had to learn it like this."

John went home. All he could remember was that the Judge had said it was bad luck for them both. It seemed to him that was a very kind thing for the Judge to say.

John did not see anything of the Judge that summer. He worked hard, planting corn and potatoes and the garden, and later he managed to hire himself out. He seemed to get jobs more easily that summer. But his family seemed to need more money. People had been impressed by Mrs. Haskell's having the doctor and Mrs. Legrand for her lying-in, and now and then they visited a little, and that meant extra money for food and tea. By working hard, though, John found himself in the fall about where he had been the preceding year.

He had put in a bid with the tannery for winter work and had had the job promised to him. Two days before he would have started, however, the Judge sent word for him to come to the big house.

The Judge made him sit down.

"John," he said, "you've kept your courage up when it must have been blamed hard. I've been thinking about you and me. I think the best thing for us both, the best way I can get my money back, is to give you another stake, if you're willing to go."

John felt that he was much nearer crying than he had been when he lost his furs. He hardly found the voice to say that he would go.

For some reason that John never understood, Seth had decided to move west in the state, so the boy had to go into the woods alone. The idea worried his mother, but he told her that in a way it would be better for him. He would be able to use Seth's cabin and work both their ranges.

But on the second day of his trip in, lying alone by his campfire, with all the miles of woods he still had to travel into, he knew that it wasn't better for him: and when at last he reached the little lake and saw Seth's cabin, he would have swapped both their ranges together for a sight of the broad brown face and the shapeless figure coming along the shore with the deceptive stride, which, like a bear's, seemed slow and shuffling but which carried him along so quickly.

He settled into Seth's cabin because it was better than his own; but there were times during that winter when he would start up because he thought he heard Seth's wild-sounding yell echoing off the pine ridge, and he would go outdoors in the darkness to listen. All through the winter, he never quite got rid of the notion that somehow Seth was going to turn up; but he never did. John never saw him again as long as he lived; but he never forgot him.

The cabin had been shut up tight. Porcupines had whittled here and there round the outside, but there was little to interest them. Seth in the woods left the ground round his cabin looking as if he had never been there. The inside of the cabin might appear to be inhabited by a pack rat, for the litter that jumbled it. But the woods Seth never spoiled the way a white man would—even John, who had picked up habits from the Indian, never learned the full art of it. Seth could spend the night and move on in the morning, and only an Indian would have known a man had slept there. It was so around his cabin.

John laid his lines out early and when the freeze came he was ready to start trapping. He followed two of the Indian's lines and laid out two new ones on his own, and after a month or so these two began to earn as well as the two others. He kept learning more and more about animals, and now and then, when he did well, he would think that Seth might have said, "Good!" the way he used to, and he could almost hear the quick laughter.

The hardest part of living alone was the Sundays without company. It was then that he realized how much Seth had done for him. The storekeeper had given him an almanac and every night before John sat down to supper, he checked off the day. That was the first reading he did, learning the look of the days of the week in print. He spent long hours puzzling over the other words and symbols and studying the picture at the head of each month. For December there was a picture of a family sitting down to dinner at a table with a white cloth, and John sometimes fancied himself as sitting in the place of the man. When things got too lonesome, he would get out that picture and think about it.

There were deep snows in February, but after the crust formed, John suddenly had a run of luck with his traps, better than anything he had had the year before, so that sometimes it was past midnight before he had finished cleaning the skins. But even so, he stayed right through to the end of the season, and then his pack was so heavy that he had to leave his traps behind.

The morning he decided to go, there was a mist over the ice on

the lake and the trees were like clouds in it. Somewhere back in the woods he heard a deer flounder in the heavy snow.

Then in the ensuing complete silence, he seemed to hear Seth's voice: "You mind Seth. *You cut two logs crossing.*" But John didn't need to be told.

The Moose River was open when he reached it, so he had to build himself a raft. He spent a full day working at it. And from that point on, he took plenty of time, when he came to the creeks, and dropped two logs over them, and made a trial trip over and back without his fur packs. It took him three days longer to come out of the woods than it had the year before, but he brought his furs with him.

The Judge saw to it that he got good prices; and when the dealer was done with the buying, John was able to pay the Judge for both stakes and for the forty-dollar loan as well. The year after that he made a clear profit for himself.

John did well in the world. He found time to learn to read and
write and handle figures. From time to time he visited the Judge,
and he found that the Judge was not a person that anyone needed
to be afraid of. When the Judge died, in John's thirtieth year,
John was owner of Freel's tannery and one of the leading men in
High Falls.

Going to the Judge's house, that day, to help settle the affairs, he thought of how scared he had been the first time he went to visit and, strangely, he remembered Seth. Without the two of them, he might never have got started in life.

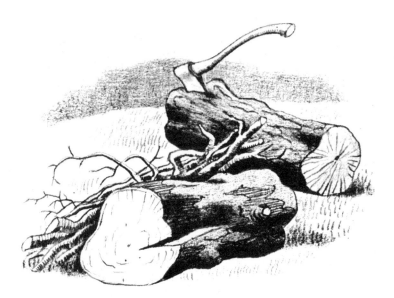

It is a simple story, this of John Haskell's, but it is not quite done. When the Judge's will was read, that afternoon, in the big house, it was found that the Judge had left the house to John, together with a good share of his timberland. There was also a sealed letter for John that the lawyer handed over.

That night in his own home, John opened the letter. It was dated the same day as the one on which John had received the money for his first pack of furs and paid the Judge. It was just a few lines long and it contained forty dollars in bills.

Dear John,

Here is the forty dollars, and I am making you a confession with it. I liked your looks when you came to me that first time. I thought you had the stuff in you. It was a dirty thing to do in a way, but I wanted to make sure of you. I never liked your father and I would never have lent him a cent. I invented that debt.

Good luck, John.